FOLLOW THAT CAR!

Stewart Carroll

STECK-VAUGHN
ELEMENTARY · SECONDARY · ADULT · LIBRARY

A Harcourt Company

www.steck-vaughn.com

ISBN 0-7398-5066-0

Copyright © 2003 Steck-Vaughn Company

Power Up! Building Reading Strength is a trademark of Steck-Vaughn Company.

Printed in China.

8 9 788 07

CONTENTS

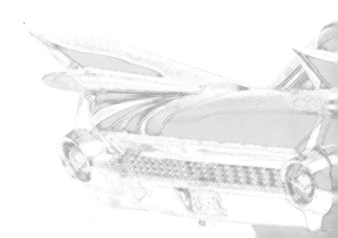

THE FIRST CARS

Cars play an important part in our lives. When cars were **invented**, they were just a new way to get places. Today, cars are used for much more. There are **vehicles** for special jobs. We feel safer when we see a police car on the street. Cabs and vans take us places. Some people drive race cars for fun. Many people choose a car because they think it looks cool.

It's hard to think of life without cars, yet we have had cars for only about a hundred years. As you read, you will learn about the history of American cars. Who made them? How were they built? Why did they change? Read on to find out about these **amazing** machines.

The Car Is Born

Who made the first car? It's hard to know. Many **inventors** tried during the 1880s and 1890s. Some people say that Karl Benz was the first. He was a German inventor. He built a car in 1886. This car did not look like today's cars. It had three wheels. It was made from a bike and a **motor.**

In the United States, the Duryea brothers had read about Karl Benz. In 1893, they made a car from a wagon. They built a motor and put it on the wagon. They called it the Motor Wagon. Three years later, the Duryea brothers made thirteen Motor Wagons. That was the beginning of the car **industry.**

Henry Ford and the Model T

An American, Henry Ford, was important to the car industry. He did not invent the first car, but he did think of better ways to make cars.

Henry Ford's Model T was called the Tin Lizzie.

Ford built the first Model T car in 1908. This car looked more like today's cars. It had four wheels and a roof. People liked the Model T so much that they gave it a special name. They called it the Tin Lizzie.

Before the Model T, cars were built one at a time. It cost a lot of money to make each one. Only a few people had the money to buy these cars.

A Better Way

In 1913, Ford thought of a better way to build cars. His workers would build them on a moving **assembly line**. In an assembly line, each worker adds one part. Workers could build each Model T quickly. It did not cost as much money to build each car. So, Ford could sell Model Ts for a low price. Many Americans bought them.

The Model T sold very well. In 19 years, Ford made more than 15 million cars. Over the years, he made the Model T better. He gave it a new motor and **headlights**.

Ford's assembly line made the **auto** industry grow. In 1914, Ford workers built three hundred thousand cars on the assembly line. In 1915, they built five hundred thousand cars. By 1925, they could build more than nine thousand cars in one day!

Ford workers build cars on an assembly line.

4

A Car for Everyone

The more quickly cars were made, the less they cost. Soon, almost every family owned a car. Some cars had new parts, or **features**. One car might carry its extra tire on the back.

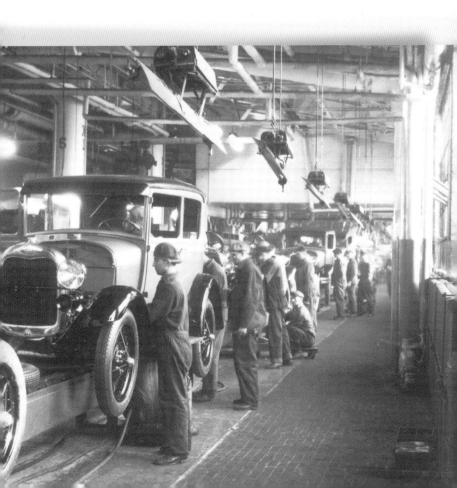

Another car might have its extra tire on the side. Most cars were black or white. The cars all looked alike, but Americans didn't mind. They were just glad to be on the road.

Americans were happy for many years. Finally, Ford sales began to slow down. Other cars had come along. These cars had parts that the Model T did not have. Some cars had a starter that worked with a key. Other cars had a horn inside. Ford had to make bigger changes. It was time to build a new car.

Ford did make another car. He called it the Model A. Many other cars were being made, too. Cars began to change.

This 1927 Model A shows Ford's new look.

CARS AND AMERICA CHANGE TOGETHER

Cars change all the time. Over the years, cars have been built to run faster. They have been made to look better. Today, cars are safer. They also **pollute** the air less than older cars.

Who makes these changes to cars? Car **designers** do. They decide how a car should look. They choose what parts to put in a car. They invent new parts to make a car better.

The next time you get into a car, think about what makes it go fast. What makes it safe? What makes it look good? What makes it pollute the air less than older cars?

Cars have come a long way since the Model T. Let's look at some of the changes.

Cars as Art

In the 1930s, people wanted cars that looked good. Designers gave cars smooth lines. Two examples of a **streamlined** car were the Chrysler Airflow and the Pierce Silver Arrow. Streamlined cars became popular during the 1930s.

Cars for World War II

In the early 1940s, America was at war. **Autoworkers** stopped making cars. Instead, they built trucks and other vehicles. A special car was invented. It was called the Jeep. People could drive it on rough land. The Jeep had no doors, so people could jump in and get out quickly. ⚡

Tail fins were an important feature on this 1959 Cadillac.

Cars for Fun

After World War II, Americans had more money. They had more free time. They wanted the best of everything.

The auto industry made cars that **customers** wanted. Designers made bigger cars. They added cool, new parts. Many cars had tail fins like a fish. The 1948 Cadillac was the first car with tail fins. Designers made tail fins bigger and bigger throughout the 1950s.

Sports Cars

By the 1960s, customers were tired of big cars. They wanted a new look. Designers gave them the sports car. Sports cars like the Pontiac GTO and the Ford Mustang were popular. The Mustang was named for a wild, fast horse.

Cars That Pollute Less

In the 1970s, American gas prices were high. Customers wanted cars that used less gas. Car designers made smaller cars. Autoworkers built **economy** cars such as the Plymouth Reliant K.

Economy cars saved gas. They were built to use gas with no **lead** in it. This gas did not pollute as much.

Cars That Are Safe

The 1980s and 1990s brought more changes. Customers cared about how safe a car was. They looked for good brakes. They wanted **airbags**. They watched how cars did in crash tests.

New laws said that cars must have seatbelts and airbags. People in the auto industry listened. They made these changes. They also added other new features that helped keep people safe.

Cars That Have It All

Today, customers still care about **safety** and economy. They also want cars that make driving easy. They want cars that pollute less. Of course, they still want great looking cars, too. ⚡

THE PAST 100 YEARS

As you have learned, American cars have changed from 1893 to now. Some changes are very important. Some are funny. Take a look. You might be surprised.

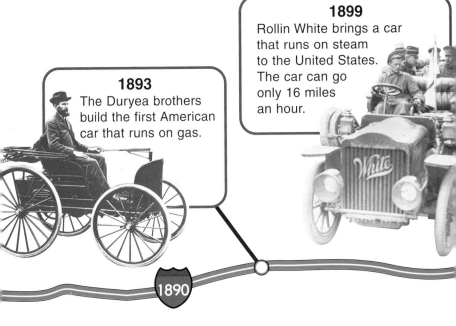

1899
Rollin White brings a car that runs on steam to the United States. The car can go only 16 miles an hour.

1893
The Duryea brothers build the first American car that runs on gas.

1890

1909
The Indianapolis Speedway opens. Car racing becomes popular. ⚡

1912
Cadillac comes out with a new way to start a motor. The driver will use a key to start the car. Before, people had to **crank** the motor to start it. Many people broke their arms or jaws while cranking a motor.

1908
Henry Ford invents the Model T. It sells for $850.

1910

1913
Henry Ford begins using the assembly line. Thousands more cars can be made each year.

1900

1900
A. L. Dyke sells cars through the mail.

13

1927
Most cars now have roofs and **windshields**.
The LaSalle V-8 is sold in many colors.

1929
Car radios are a
new feature.

1925
Designer Charles
Kettering uses a new
paint for General
Motors cars. The new
paint dries very fast.
Workers can paint a
car in one hour. It
used to take them
thirty days!

1931
The Marmon 16 can
go up to one hundred
miles an hour. It is
lighter than most cars.

1920

1930

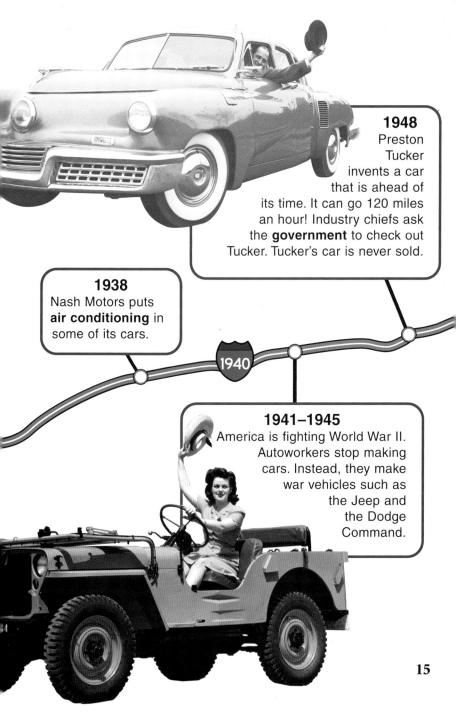

1948
Preston Tucker invents a car that is ahead of its time. It can go 120 miles an hour! Industry chiefs ask the **government** to check out Tucker. Tucker's car is never sold.

1938
Nash Motors puts **air conditioning** in some of its cars.

1940

1941–1945
America is fighting World War II. Autoworkers stop making cars. Instead, they make war vehicles such as the Jeep and the Dodge Command.

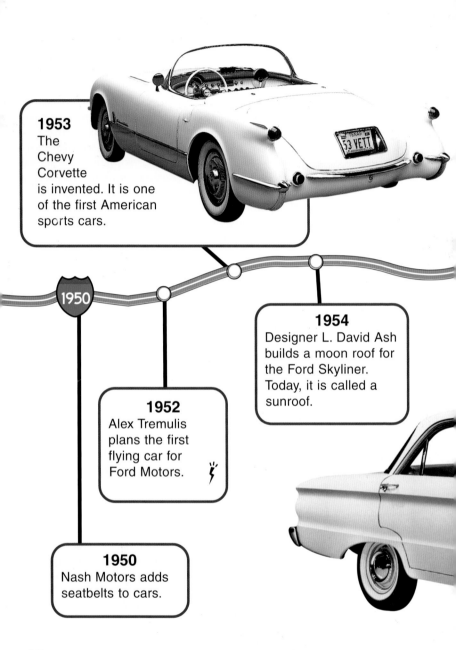

1953
The Chevy Corvette is invented. It is one of the first American sports cars.

1950

1954
Designer L. David Ash builds a moon roof for the Ford Skyliner. Today, it is called a sunroof.

1952
Alex Tremulis plans the first flying car for Ford Motors.

1950
Nash Motors adds seatbelts to cars.

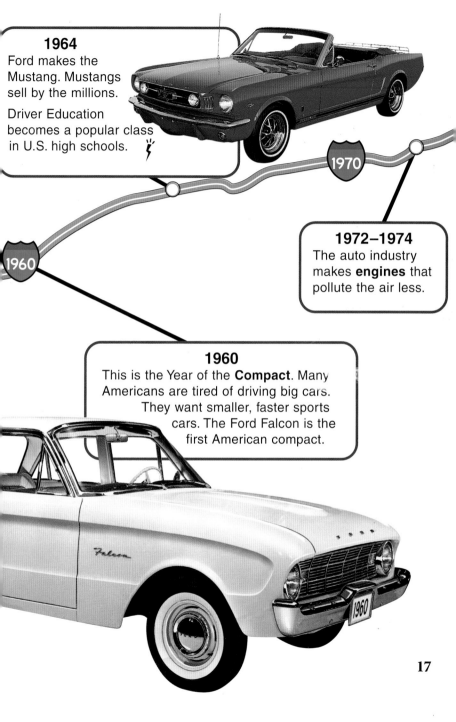

1964
Ford makes the Mustang. Mustangs sell by the millions.

Driver Education becomes a popular class in U.S. high schools.

1970

1972–1974
The auto industry makes **engines** that pollute the air less.

1960

1960
This is the Year of the **Compact**. Many Americans are tired of driving big cars. They want smaller, faster sports cars. The Ford Falcon is the first American compact.

17

1986
Driver airbags are placed in all Ford Tempo and Ford Topaz cars. There is a waiting list of people who want to buy these cars.

1980

1980
Digital numbers are used in car clocks. They also show speed and how much gas is in the car tank.

A **computer chip** is put in some car engines. It helps an engine work better.

1983
Sport **utility** vehicles become popular. Today, they are called SUVs.

18

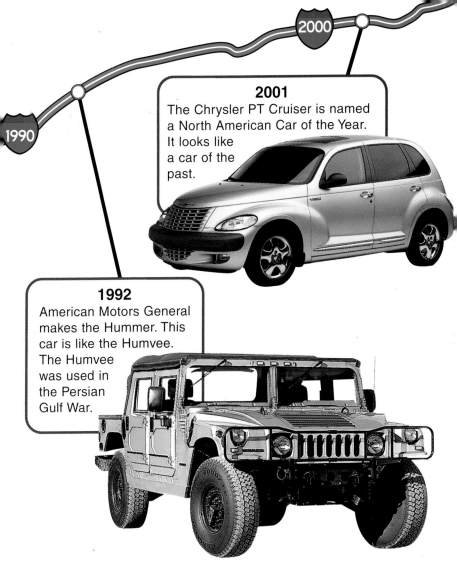

2000

2001
The Chrysler PT Cruiser is named a North American Car of the Year. It looks like a car of the past.

1990

1992
American Motors General makes the Hummer. This car is like the Humvee. The Humvee was used in the Persian Gulf War.

You've learned about many changes made to American cars. Will cars keep changing? Turn the page to find out about cars of the future.

WHICH WAY TO THE FUTURE?

Cars have changed over the years. We used to crank a car's motor. Now we crank up its air conditioning. What will the future bring? How much more can cars change?

What Fuel Will We Use?

Think about how different today's cars are from cars of the past. Will cars use gas fifty years from now? What would happen if we used up all the gas? What **fuel** could we use to make cars run? Car designers think about these questions all the time.

Designers know that today's cars still have problems. Designers are working on cars that will run better and pollute less.

The GM Sunrayer gets its power from the sun. ▶

An **electric** car would pollute less, but not many people want an electric car. The electric car uses some gas. It also uses **batteries**. The batteries are heavy. They don't last very long. Also, the electric car is slower than a car that runs on gas.

A car that uses **solar power** would also pollute less. In 1987, the GM Sunraycer was tested. The Sunraycer runs on batteries that use the sun's heat. These batteries cost a lot of money. We will probably not see cars that run on solar power for many years.

More Changes

You've learned about electric cars and cars that use solar power. Designers are working on other ideas, too. Some cars use **satellites**. A satellite helps a driver with many things. If you lock your keys inside the car, the satellite can unlock the car. If you are lost or your car breaks down, the satellite can call for help. A satellite may even stop an **accident**. It can tell the car to slow down or stop. The satellite can keep many **passengers** safe.

This car has a satellite map.

Cars Will Still Be Around

America loves cars. Of course, there are other ways to get places. People could ride on subways, buses, or trains. Americans probably won't give up their cars, though. They like to just pick up the keys and go.

Cars will change. In years to come, car designers will make cars even better. Future cars might use solar power. They might even fly. It will be fun to see how cars change in the future. ⚡

GLOSSARY

accident (AK suh duhnt) *noun* An accident is something that you do not plan to have happen. It is often something bad.

airbags (EHR bagz) *noun* Airbags pop out inside a car during a crash to keep riders safe.

air conditioning (EHR kuhn dihsh uhn ihng) *noun* Air conditioning cools the air inside a building or car.

amazing (uh MAYZ ihng) *adjective* Something that is surprising or wonderful is amazing.

assembly line (uh SEHM blee LYN) *noun* An assembly line is a moving belt like the ones you see at the store. The belt is used to move things. Each worker adds a different part to the thing.

auto (AWT oh) *adjective* Auto is another word for car. Auto is short for automobile.

autoworkers (AWT oh wur kuhrz) *noun* Autoworkers are people who build cars.

batteries (BAT uhr eez) *noun* Batteries are things that store power. They help a car start.

compact (KAHM pakt) *noun* A compact is a small car.

computer chip (kuhm PYOOT uhr CHIHP) *noun*
A computer chip is a tiny circle or square that holds information.

crank (KRAYNK) *verb* To crank means to turn a handle.

customers (KUHS tuh muhrz) *noun* Customers are people who shop for and buy things.

designers (dih ZYN uhrs) *noun* Designers are people whose job is to draw a plan. Designers make things look or work better.

digital (DIHJ ih tuhl) *adjective* Digital is a way of showing numbers on something such as a watch or a clock.

economy (ih KAHN uh mee) *adjective* Economy means using less of something.

electric (ee LEHK trihk) *adjective* Electric means using electricity.

engines (EHN juhnz) *noun* Engines are machines that make cars run.

features (FEE chuhrz) *noun* Features are special parts of a thing, such as the door or color of a car.

fuel (FYOO uhl) *noun* Fuel is a liquid or solid that makes things move. Cars use gas for fuel.

government (GUHV uhrn muhnt) *noun* Government is a group that makes laws.

headlights (HEHD lyts) *noun* Headlights are the front lights of a car that light up the road at night.

industry (IHN duhs tree) *noun* An industry is a group that makes something to sell.

invented (ihn VEHN tehd) *adjective* Something that has been invented has been thought about and then made for the first time.

inventors (ihn VEHN tuhrz) *noun* Inventors are people who think of new ideas and make new things.

lead (LEHD) *noun* Lead is a type of metal.

motor (MOHT uhr) *noun* A motor is a machine that makes something move.

passengers (PAS uhn juhrz) *noun* Passengers are people who ride in a car, truck, bus, or van.

pollute (puh LOOT) *verb* To pollute is to make something dirty, such as the air or water.

power (POW uhr) *noun* Power makes machines run.

safety (SAYF tee) *noun* Safety is being safe from getting hurt.

satellites (SAT uhl yts) *noun* Satellites move around Earth and send messages from one place to another. Satellites are used for some TVs and cars and to take pictures in space.

solar (SOH luhr) *adjective* Solar is heat and light from the sun.

streamlined (STREEM lynd) *adjective* Streamlined means having smooth lines. Something that is streamlined can move quickly.

utility (yoo TIHL uh tee) *adjective* Utility means that something is useful. A Sport Utility Vehicle is useful on rough roads, rocky ground, and in mud.

vehicles (VEE uh kuhlz) *noun* Vehicles are things that people drive or ride in.

windshields (WIHND sheeldz) *noun* Windshields are glass on the front of cars. They stop wind, rain, and dust from getting into the cars.

INDEX